# A Note to Parents

For many children, learnii _____ "I hate math!" is their first response _____ silently add "Me, too!" Children often see adults comfortably reading and writing, but they rarely have such models for mathematics. And math fear can be catching!

The easy-to-read stories in this *Hello Math* series were written to give children a positive introduction to mathematics and parents a pleasurable re-acquaintance with a subject that is important to everyone's life. *Hello Math* stories make mathematical ideas accessible, interesting, and fun for children. The activities and suggestions at the end of each book provide parents with a hands-on approach to help children develop mathematical interest and confidence.

### Enjoy the mathematics!
• Give your child a chance to retell the story. The more familiar children are with the story, the more they will understand its mathematical concepts.
• Use the colorful illustrations to help children "hear and see" the math at work in the story.
• Treat the math activities as games to be played for fun. Follow your child's lead. Spend time on those activities that engage your child's interest and curiosity.
• Activities, especially ones using physical materials, help make abstract mathematical ideas concrete.

Learning is a messy process and learning about math calls for children to become immersed in lively experiences that help them make sense of mathematical concepts and symbols.

Although learning about numbers is basic to math, other ideas, such as identifying shapes and patterns, measuring, collecting and interpreting data, reasoning logically, and thinking about chance are also important. By reading these stories and having fun with the activities, you will help your child enthusiastically say "*Hello, Math*," instead of "I hate math."

— Marilyn Burns
National Mathematics Educator
Author of *The I Hate Mathematics! Book*

TURTLES
$20.⁰⁰
each

*Dedicated to Samtoo, Manny, and Moe*
*— best pets and true companions*
*— J.R.*

*For Casey and Matthew*
*— M.J.*

Copyright © 1995 by Scholastic Inc.
The activities on pages 44–48 copyright © 1995 by Marilyn Burns.
All rights reserved. Published by Scholastic Inc.
HELLO READER!, CARTWHEEL BOOKS, and the
CARTWHEEL BOOKS logo are registered trademarks of Scholastic Inc.

Library of Congress Cataloging-in-Publication Data

Rocklin, Joanne.
How much is that guinea pig in the window? / by Joanne Rocklin ; illustrated by Meredith Johnson.
p.   cm.— (Hello math reader. Level 4)
"Cartwheel Books."
Summary: Mr. Day's fourth-grade class has a contest, recycling bottles and cans so that they will have enough money to buy a guinea pig.
ISBN 0-590-22716-5
[1. Schools — Fiction.  2. Contests — Fiction.  3. Recycling (Waste) — Fiction.  4. Guinea pigs — Fiction.]   I. Johnson, Meredith, ill. II. Title.   III. Series.
PZ7.R59Ho 1995
[Fic] — dc20                                              95-13231
                                                            CIP
                                                            AC

12  11  10  9  8  7  6  5  4  3          5  6  7  8  9/9  0/0

Printed in the U.S.A.                                        23

First Scholastic printing, October 1995

# How Much Is That Guinea Pig in the Window?

by Joanne Rocklin

Illustrated by Meredith Johnson

## Hello Math — Level 4

SCHOLASTIC INC.

New York  Toronto  London  Auckland  Sydney

# CHAPTER ONE

# The Nicest Teacher in the World

One Monday morning Mr. Day said, "We have fifty dollars from the bake sale. That is enough money for a class pet."

"HOORAY!" shouted the class.

"You're the nicest teacher in the school!" said Nora.

"In the world!" said Amy.

"PHOOEY!" said Brad. "Who wants a smelly old pet?

"Fifty dollars can buy a small TV. Fifty dollars can buy lots of baseball cards. Fifty dollars can buy a Mighty Magic Robot."

"Let's vote," said Mr. Day. "Who wants a pet?"

"PHOOEY!" said Brad.

That morning Mr. Day's class went to Mrs. Piper's Pet Palace.

"Look! The iguana is on sale," said Sam. "But its cage costs too much," said Lily.

"Let's get a tarantula!" said Brad.

"Bunnies!" cried Sally.

"Two for sixty dollars. Too bad we don't have enough money."

"We can buy just one bunny," said Eric.

"But what if the two bunnies are best friends?" asked Sally.

"How about a whole family of mice?" asked Karen.

"Maybe frogs are a better deal," said Peter.

"We can buy two turtles," said Sam.

"Let's fill up the classroom with crickets and worms!" said Brad.

"How long is the snake?" asked Emma.

"It is three feet long," said Mrs. Piper.

"That snake costs $20 a foot," said Emma.

"Do you have a shorter snake?"

"Sorry," said Mrs. Piper.

Jon was a new student in the class.
"A dog would be a good friend to have,"
he said. "Are the puppies half price?"

"Sorry," said Mrs. Piper.

"What about a tarantula?" asked Brad.

Suddenly there was a terrible scream. "HELP! LET ME OUT OF HERE!"

"A talking parrot!" said Mike. "What a great pet for our class!"

"We would need to have many bake sales to buy that bird," Sally said.

"It's hard to choose the best pet," said Tom.

"It's not hard!" said Amy. "Here is a riddle for you.

I am small and soft and smart.

I am the right price.

I do not need to go for a walk.

My name says pig but I do not say oink.

What pet am I?"

"A guinea pig!" said Jon.

GUINEA
PIGS
$35.ᵒᵒ each
CAGE
$15.ᵒᵒ

"Let's vote," said Mr. Day.

"PHOOEY!" said Brad.

"HOORAY!" shouted the rest of the class.

"We will come back to buy the guinea pig next week," Mr. Day said to Mrs. Piper.

"But we have enough money to buy it today!" said Rob.

"What about guinea pig food?" asked Mr. Day.

The children looked in their backpacks.

Jon found one nickel and two dimes.

Lily found five nickels.

Emma found a quarter.

"Not enough," said Amy.

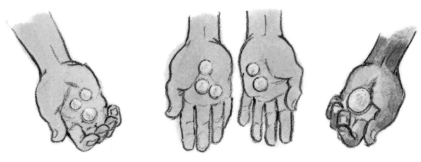

"We can all bring some money from home," said Nora.

"That's too easy," said Mr. Day. "I want you to work for the money."

"Work! PHOOEY!" said Brad. "Who said Mr. Day is the nicest teacher in the world?"

# CHAPTER TWO

# Money from Garbage

"What kind of work can we do?"
asked Emma.

"Here is another riddle," said Mr. Day.
"This work can get five dollars. This work
can clean up your neighborhood. This work
can make money from garbage."

"How can we make money from garbage?" asked Brad. "We can't do magic tricks!"

"I get it!" said Nora. "It's not a magic trick. We can find empty bottles and cans. We can take them to the recycling center. The recycling center will pay five cents for each one."

"I will tell you exactly how many nickels we need to get five dollars," said Rob. "One nickel and another nickel makes ten cents and another nickel makes fifteen cents…"

"Wait!" said Amy. "There are twenty nickels in one dollar."

"And we need five dollars," said Eric.

"And five times twenty nickels is one hundred nickels!" said Emma.

Rob jumped up from his chair. "That means we need to find—"

"ONE HUNDRED BOTTLES AND CANS!" shouted the whole class.

"I know this class can do it by next
Monday," said Mr. Day.
"Everybody choose one person to make
a team."

"How about a contest?" asked Amy.

"Yes!" cried Eric and Rob.

"The winners could be the first guinea pig monitors," said Nora.

Jon said nothing. Brad said nothing.

"I guess we could be a team," said Jon.

"It will take magic to win," said Brad.

Each day the teams brought their empty
bottles and cans to school.

On Tuesday, Sally and Eric went
to the beach. They found
five cans,
four bottles,
two pairs of sunglasses,
three sun hats,
and one lost dog.

Mike and Tom worked hard on
Wednesday. They telephoned
two grandfathers,
one grandmother,
two aunts,
and one uncle.
They picked up bottles and cans
from their families.

Sam and Lily worked hard in Lily's
mother's ice cream shop. They found
eleven bottles and nine cans.

Brad did not work hard.

"PHOOEY!" he said.

"Lily's mother owns an ice cream shop.

Lily and Sam will win!

I am going to play in the park."

PUPPIES

GUINEA
PIGS
$35.⁰⁰
each

Every afternoon Jon went to the pet store.
He helped Mrs. Piper with the guinea pigs.
He liked a frisky, brown one the best.

On Thursday afternoon Mr. Day said,
"We need to check our chart.
Let's count the bottles and cans."

"Put all the bottles here," said Nora,
"and all the cans there. Then we will count
them."

"It's okay to mix up the bottles and
cans!" said Amy.
"One, two, three, four, five,
six, seven, eight, nine…"

"I have a good idea!" said Nora.

"I'll make a tally mark for every one you count."

"Try it like this," said Jon.

Soon all the bottles and cans were counted. Rob looked happy. "This class is more than halfway there!"

But Jon was worried.

That afternoon a man bought two guinea pigs.

"Guinea pigs always sell quickly," said Mrs. Piper.

Jon was afraid the brown guinea pig would sell quickly, too!

# CHAPTER THREE
# A Great Idea

Nora went to Amy's house on Friday.
"Next week my big sister is having
a birthday party," said Amy.
"There will be pizza
and cake
and two cans of soda
for each guest."

"And we will get all the empty soda
cans!" said Nora.

Amy and Nora counted the cans of soda:
six grape,
six cola,
six lemon-lime,
six strawberry,
six root beer,
six pineapple-peach.

"I am very, very thirsty," said Amy.

"Me, too," said Nora.

"Let's each drink one of the sodas now," said Amy.

Amy chose root beer.
Nora chose lemon-lime.
*GLUG GLUG GLUG!*

"Mmm. Delicious!" said Amy.

"Delicious!" said Nora.

"I am still thirsty," said Amy.

"Me, too," said Nora.

"My grandmother is coming to the party.
She doesn't drink soda," said Amy.
"Let's drink Grandmother's sodas."
Amy chose strawberry.
Nora chose pineapple-peach.
*GLUG GLUG GLUGGEDY GLUG!*
"Burp!" went Amy.
"Burp!" went Nora.
The girls were not thirsty anymore.
"On Monday our class will count the
bottles and cans again," said Amy.
"Too bad my sister's party is on Tuesday."
"I have a great idea!" said Nora.
Amy and Nora found 36 cups.
They poured 18 cans of soda
into those cups.

"I can't wait!" said Amy.

"Let's empty every single can.

Then we will be the top team!"

Amy found some empty pots.

She poured one can of pineapple-peach

into a small pot,

and two cans of cola into a medium pot,

and five cans of grape soda

into a big spaghetti pot.

Now there were six cans left.

Amy poured them into a giant bowl.

Amy and Nora tasted the soda.

"Mmm. Delicious!" said Amy.

"Delicious!" said Nora.

"I have another great idea!"

Soon Amy's big sister came home.

"We have a riddle for you," said Amy.

"It is the best drink in the world.

It is grape, cola, lemon-lime,

strawberry, root beer, and pineapple-peach.

It is in the swimming pool.

What is it?"

"I give up," said Amy's sister.

"SODA PUNCH!" said Amy.

"What?" shouted her sister.

"Please taste it," said Nora.

Amy's sister tasted the soda punch.

"Mmm. Delicious!" she said.

"It IS the best drink in the world!"

## CHAPTER FOUR
# The Promise

On Saturday, Jon said to Brad,
"Come to Mrs. Piper's Pet Palace with me.
I want to show you something special."

There were only three guinea pigs left.
Jon picked up the brown one.
He hugged it.
Brad hugged the guinea pig, too.

Jon helped the guinea pig do a trick.
Then the guinea pig did a little dance.
"That guinea pig is smart!" said Brad.
Brad fed it a carrot stick.

"The guinea pig likes you," said Jon.
"I like the guinea pig," said Brad.

A girl was in the pet store, too.
She bought six mice, two rabbits,
one puppy, one iguana, and one tarantula.

"Where will you keep all those pets?"
asked Jon.

"I live in a very big house," said the girl.
"And I want those three guinea pigs, too."

"Oh, no!" said Brad. "That brown guinea
pig belongs to our class."

"It does not!" said the girl.

"We were going to buy it on Monday,"
said Jon.

"I am here to buy it today," said the girl.
"I want that dancing guinea pig!"

"I will not sell the brown guinea pig
until Monday," said Mrs. Piper.

"Let's get to work!" shouted Brad.

Brad and Jon ran to the park.
They found eleven cans and one bottle
in the trash.
Then they played ball together.
They found nine more cans and three more
bottles on Sunday.
Then they went to Jon's house to play.

On Monday morning it was time to
count the bottles and cans again.

"Let's group them by twos," said Mike.

"Yes," said Rob. "Put them in pairs."

"But we have too many," said Karen.
"There will be pairs all over the room.
Even in the hall!"

"No, no," said Sam. "Make groups of fives!"

"Why don't we count by tens?" said Emma.

"Let's vote," said Brad.

Soon all the bottles and cans were counted.

"We have more than enough!" shouted Nora.

"HOORAY!" shouted the class.

Mr. Day grinned.

"A guinea pig likes to eat," he said.

"We will have to keep recycling all year."

"EASY!" shouted Brad.
"Guinea pig, here we come!"

That morning Mr. Day's class went to the recycling center with the bottles and cans.

That afternoon the class went to Mrs. Piper's Pet Palace.

"You have enough money for food for one month," said Mrs. Piper.
"You have enough money for other things, too. I will give you everything for half price because Jon helped me with the guinea pigs."

"You are the best pet store owner in the world!" said Amy.

Just then the girl came into the store.

"I want that dancing guinea pig!" she said.

"Sorry," said Mrs. Piper.

"The guinea pig belongs to Mr. Day's class."

"HELP! LET ME OUT OF HERE!"
yelled the parrot.

"Can I buy that parrot?" asked the girl.

"Sold!" said Mrs. Piper.

Sam turned to Jon.

"Will you help Lily and me take care
of the guinea pig?" Sam asked.

"Okay," said Jon. "But I want
Brad to help, too. We're a team."

"Maybe we were not the best team," said
Brad, "but we sure are best friends!"

# • ABOUT THE ACTIVITIES •

Yours is not to question why; just invert and multiply. This sums up many adults' experiences learning arithmetic. But for children today, doing arithmetic has to expand beyond memorizing facts and doing paper-and-pencil computations to include estimating, figuring mentally, and solving problems. The goal is: think, reason, and explain why your answer makes sense.

The activities and games in this section involve children with arithmetic. The directions are written for you to read along with your child. Some children are intrigued by numbers, find them easy to understand, and enjoy numerical challenges; other children are not particularly drawn to numbers and are reluctant to tackle numerical problems. The problems in this section are intended to invite interest and draw children into thinking about numbers, not to test them or make them feel inadequate.

Children may enjoy doing their favorite activities again and again. Encourage them to do so. Or try a different activity at each reading. Also, there's no one way that's best to solve the problems. Be curious about how your child reasons. And have fun with math!

— Marilyn Burns

You'll find tips and suggestions
for guiding the activities whenever
you see a box like this!

# Chapter One

Mr. Day's students did a lot of figuring to spend $50. See if you can solve these problems.

Sam noticed that the iguana was on sale, half-off of $70. Why couldn't the class buy it?

How much would one bunny cost?

Frogs cost three for $10. Mice cost two for $5. Which costs more: one frog or one mouse? Explain how you reasoned.

The snake cost $20 a foot. How long a snake could the class buy for $50?

How would you spend the $50 in the pet store?

## Chapter Two

Rob, Amy, Eric, and Emma figured out that 100 nickels makes $5. How do you know this is true?

On Tuesday, Sally and Eric found five cans and four bottles. How much money would they get for them? Sam and Lily found eleven bottles and nine cans. How much money would they get?

# Chapter Three

For her birthday party, Amy's sister had these sodas: six grape, six cola, six lemon-lime, six strawberry, six root beer, and six pineapple-peach. How many cans were there altogether? How many cans did Amy drink? How many did Nora drink?

What do you think about the punch Amy and Nora made? Write a recipe for your favorite punch.

## Chapter Four

In the pet store, a girl bought six mice, two rabbits, one puppy, one iguana, and one tarantula. How much did these pets cost altogether?

On Saturday, Brad and Jon found eleven cans and one bottle. How much money did Brad and Jon earn for the class?

Mrs. Piper gives the class half-off on some things for the guinea pig. How much would it cost to buy all the items on sale?

How much would it cost to buy the guinea pig food for the whole year? How many bottles and cans would it take to get that money?